HAPPY HANUKAH!

To: _____

From: _____

Date: _____

Grateful acknowledgment is made to BMG Chrysalis Company for permission to reprint "Honeyky Hanukah" by Woody Guthrie.
Text © 2003 Woody Guthrie Publications, Inc. (BMI). All Rights Administered by BUG Music, Inc.,
a BMG Chrysalis company. Used by Permission. All Rights Reserved.

Visit us on the Web! randomhouse.com/kids

Educators and librarians, for a variety of teaching tools, visit us at RHTeachersLibrarians.com

Library of Congress Cataloging-in-Publication Data
Guthrie, Woody.
Honeyky Hanukah / Woody Guthrie, Dave Horowitz. — First edition.
pages cm.
Summary: A family celebrates Hanukkah with latkes, hugs, kisses, and dancing.
ISBN 978-0-385-37926-7 (trade) — ISBN 978-0-375-97339-0 (lib. bdg.) — ISBN 978-0-375-98239-2 (ebook)
1. Children's songs, English—United States—Texts. [1. Hanukkah—Songs and music. 2. Songs.] I. Horowitz, Dave, illustrator. II. Title.
PZ8.3.G9635Ho 2014 782.42083—dc23 [E] 2013045762

The illustrations for this book were created with construction paper, charcoal, and colored pencils.
Book design by Nicole de las Heras

MANUFACTURED IN CHINA
10 9 8 7 6 5 4 3 2 1
First Edition

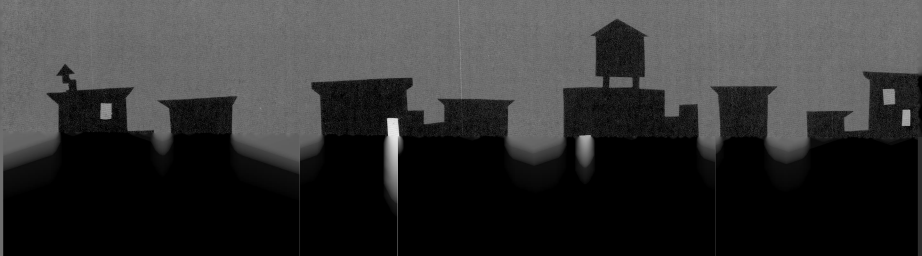

WOODY GUTHRIE
HONEYKY HANUKAH

pictures by Dave Horowitz

Doubleday Books for Young Readers

It's Honeyky Hanukah 'round and around,
Honeycake Hanukah, eat them down,

Latkes and goody things all over town,
It's Honeyky Hanukah time.

It's Honeyky Hanukah, shaky my hand,
My candles are burning all over this land,

To light the dark road for the man passing by,
It's Honeyky Hanukah time.

It's Honeyky Hanukah, kissy my cheek,
The light in my window, it burns for a week,

It's Honeyky Hanukah, makes me feel glad,
This box for Mother and this box for Dad,

For sister and brother, nice ribbons I'll tie,
It's Honeyky Hanukah time.

It's Honeyky Hanukah, huggy me tight,
It's Hanukah day, and it's Hanukah night,

If you've got no money, well, that's all right,
It's Honeyky Hanukah time.

It's Honeyky Hanukah, kiss me some more,
We'll sing and go dancing around on the floor,

Your kiss is nicer than cakes from the store,
It's Honeyky Hanukah time.

It's Honeyky Hanukah, brushy my hair,
Let's dance a big hora and jump in the air,

You look lots prettier to me every year
At Honeyky Hanukah time.

A Coney Island Hanukah:
Woody Guthrie's New York Story

Woody Guthrie's Jewish songs can be traced to his friendship with his mother-in-law, Aliza Greenblatt, a well-known Yiddish poet who lived down the street from Woody and his family in Coney Island, New York, in the 1940s. Woody and Aliza often discussed their artistic projects and critiqued each other's work, finding common ground in their shared love for culture and social justice. Here is the story of how their unlikely collaboration began.

In 1942, Sophie Maslow, a dancer who had performed with the Martha Graham Dance Company, choreographed a suite for the New Dance Group using some of Woody's songs. She and Marjorie Mazia, another dancer with the troupe, went to Woody's Greenwich Village apartment to invite him to perform at the premiere. According to Guthrie family legend, Marjorie and Woody fell in love during the rehearsals. They moved to Coney Island in June 1943 to be near Marjorie's parents, Aliza and Isadore Greenblatt.

Aliza played a major role in the Guthrie family's life. Known as Bubbie (the Yiddish word for *grandma*), Aliza cared for her grandchildren and held Friday-night Sabbath dinners. Woody saw a strong connection between the Jewish struggle and that of his fellow Oklahomans during the

Dust Bowl, and was inspired to write songs that celebrated Jewish culture. He performed his Hanukah songs at local Jewish community centers and wrote other songs about Jewish history, spiritual life, World War II, and the anti-fascist cause.

At the bottom of the handwritten lyrics for "Honeyky Hanukah," Woody signed:

Woody Guthrie
3520 Mermaid Avenue
Brooklyn, 24, New York
November 21, 1949

Woody Guthrie lived in Coney Island for seven years. The songs he wrote there—full of his love for family and home—convey to us today the stories of a bygone time.

Woody and Marjorie Mazia Guthrie, circa 1944

This book belongs to

_____

THE UGLY DUCKLING

Adapted by Mary Packard from the original
TIMELESS TALES FROM HALLMARK™ story

LANDOLL'S
Ashland, Ohio 44805

A very long time ago, in a beautiful meadow, a mother duck sat on her nest waiting for her ducklings to hatch.

Crack! Crack! Crack, Crack, Crack! The mother duck squawked in excitement as, one by one, five fuzzy yellow ducks emerged from their eggs.

"Oh, my babies!" the mother duck quacked as she nuzzled the ducklings and held them close to her. But the ducklings had no time for hugs.

"Hi, Mom! Can you teach us to swim?" asked one little duckling.

"How about flying?" asked another.

"I want to fly and dive," said another.

The mother duck laughed and said, "Swimming first!"

But just as the mother duck turned to lead her five little ducklings to the pond, she looked back at their nest. "Oh, dear!" she said. "You still have another brother or sister who hasn't hatched yet."

"We don't want to wait. We want to swim!" said all five ducklings at once.

"What is all the squawking about?" asked a nosy old duck who waddled by.

"I'm sorry, it's just my children," said the mother.

"Are they all hatched?" asked the old duck.

"Almost," said the mother.

The old duck looked at the remaining egg and said, "But, my dear, that doesn't look like one of ours."

"It most certainly is!" said the mother duck.

"No need to get huffy," said the old duck. "Why don't you just leave that egg? You already have five beautiful ducklings."

Before the mother could argue with the old duck, her ducklings quacked in fright, "Mother! Mother! Look!"

The frightened ducklings pointed to the nest, where a brand-new duckling sat with an eggshell on its head. This duckling did not look at all like the others. He was big, and his feathers were a different color.

"Oh, my dear!" quacked the old duck. "I think there's been a mistake. That simply cannot be your child."

"Well, he is my child," snapped the mother duck. "Don't worry," she whispered into the ugly duckling's ear, "by tomorrow you'll be just as soft and yellow as my other ducklings."

The next morning the five yellow ducklings woke up early, eager to start their day.

"May we go swimming today, Mother?" one duckling begged.

"Yes, please, Mother," said another. "You promised!"

The mother duck smiled. "Of course," she said happily. "Follow me to the pond, children."

The ugly duckling, who had not turned soft and yellow like the others, followed his brothers and sisters to the water. Then he jumped in, splashing and swimming circles around everyone.

The other ducklings were not happy. They refused to let the ugly duckling swim with them. Instead, they made him follow behind all by himself.

When other bird families came to the pond and saw the ugly duckling, they made fun of him.

"That large duckling is such a homely creature!" whispered a drake, as he and his family swam by.

"I beg your pardon," said the mother duck haughtily, "but all of my children are beautiful to me."

Later, two other ducks began to tease the ugly duckling and peck at his feathers. Before the mother duck noticed, the ugly duckling's brothers and sisters had joined in.

"Shoo! Shoo!" the mother duck shouted furiously at the intruders. "And as for you," she added, turning to the ducklings, "I'm ashamed of you all! How could you be so mean to your own brother?"

But the yellow ducklings were not sorry for the way they had acted. They were embarrassed by their strange-looking brother, and they wished he would play somewhere else.

As the months passed and winter approached, all the ducklings grew. Unfortunately, the ugly duckling grew even bigger and uglier.

The mother duck gathered her children together to prepare them to fly south. "It's time for you to be off on your own," she said. "I hope we will all meet back at the pond next summer."

When it came time to fly off, the other ducklings decided to trick the ugly duckling.

"Let's go in separate directions," suggested one of the brothers. "He won't know which one of us to follow."

"Good idea," agreed one of the sisters. "Then we'll all meet later and fly south together without him."

And so the ugly duckling was abandoned by his brothers and sisters. He tried to find other ducks to fly south with, but no one wanted to be his friend.

"I guess I'll just have to find my own way," said the ugly duckling, trying to hold back his tears. And he set off by foot on his journey alone.

He wandered through the woods for days. It began to snow, and the ugly duckling grew tired. He sat down, laying his head against a log to rest. Just then, a nearby door opened, and out hopped a little rabbit.

"My name is Runabout," said the rabbit. "Who are you, and what are you doing here?"

"They call me 'Ugly,'" replied the duckling. "I'm resting, but I'll understand if you want me to move along."

"You won't get very far in this weather," said Runabout. "Besides, it's too late to fly south. Why don't you wait out the winter in my house?"

No one but his mother had ever been nice to him before. "Are you sure?" asked the ugly duckling.

"Of course!" Runabout promised. "Come on in!"

So the ugly duckling went into the rabbit's house and settled down for a nice, warm nap. Soon they heard a dinner bell.

"I hope you like carrot soup," said Runabout.

"I'm so hungry I could eat anything!" said the ugly duckling.

Runabout led the ugly duckling through a maze of tunnels until they arrived in the dining room, where all the rabbits ate together.

"What's he doing here?" asked the head rabbit.

"I invited him," said Runabout proudly. "He's my guest."

"Well, he can't stay," said the head rabbit. "Only rabbits are allowed at this table."

Runabout begged the other rabbits to let the ugly duckling stay, but they refused.

Runabout told the ugly duckling how very sorry he was.

"It's all right," said the ugly duckling. "Thank you for being my friend today."

"I'll always be your friend," said Runabout.

The two friends said good-bye, and the ugly duckling went on his way. The wind grew colder and colder as the ugly duckling wandered through the woods.

"I wish I could have stayed with Runabout," he said. "For the first time, I really felt like I belonged somewhere."

The ugly duckling did not know that two hungry alligators had overheard him.

The alligators introduced themselves, and one said, "Come home with us. We have a place where you could belong."

"We'll be your friends forever," promised the other.

The ugly duckling certainly needed friends and a warm place to stay, so he followed the alligators through a spooky swamp to their home.

But when the alligators set the table for two and then placed him on a platter, the ugly duckling became very suspicious.

"I want to leave now," quacked the ugly duckling.

"Not so soon, my little friend," said the first alligator. "We haven't eaten yet, and you're the main course!"

Luckily for the ugly duckling, Runabout had been following his tracks. The brave rabbit rushed into the house, hopped right up on the table, and knocked the platter off. The ugly duckling flew out the open window before the alligators could catch him. Runabout was right behind him.

Safely outside, the ugly duckling turned to Runabout and said, "You saved my life. You are a true friend."

Runabout smiled. Then the two friends said good-bye again, and the ugly duckling continued on his journey.

The long, cold winter passed, and spring finally returned. One bright, warm day, the ugly duckling went for a swim in a shimmering stream. Ahead of him two swans swam gracefully across the water. The ugly duckling hoped they wouldn't see him.

"I'm so ugly," he thought. But as he bent his head to hide from their view, he caught a glimpse of his reflection in the water.

"Who is that handsome swan?" he wondered.

The ugly duckling spread his magnificent wings and arched his long, graceful neck.

"It's me!" he said joyfully. "I'm a beautiful swan!"

The other swans glided over to greet him. They thought he was the grandest swan of all, and they asked him to be the leader of their flock.

"Of course, I would be honored," answered the ugly duckling, who was no longer ugly and not a duckling at all! And so, the handsome swan swam off with the other swans and lived happily ever after. Finally, he had found a place where he belonged.

Manufactured in U.S.A.

First Edition 10 9 8 7 6 5 4 3 2
ISBN 1-56987-217-1

Prepared and Distributed by Landoll, Inc.
425 Orange St. • Ashland, Ohio 44805

Designed by Antler & Baldwin Design Group • Developed by Nancy Hall, Inc.
Illustrations by Vaccaro Associates, Inc. • Painted by Lou Paleno